Little Charmers

W9-ARX-058

CHARMER GIRLS ROCK!

Adapted by Meredith Rusu
from the teleplay by Steve Sullivan

SCHOLASTIC INC.

Published by Scholastic Inc., *Publishers since 1920.* SCHOLASTIC and associated logos
are trademarks and/or registered trademarks of Scholastic Inc.

The publisher does not have any control over and does not assume
any responsibility for author or third-party websites or their content.

Scholastic UK, Coventry, Warwickshire

ISBN 978-1-338-03730-2

10 9 8 7 6 5 4 3 2 1   16 17 18 19 20

Printed in China

First printing 2016

Book design by Erin McMahon

It was a sunny day in Charmville.
The Little Charmers were happy.
Posie had won an award at school!
"How about some charm cheer for our
champion!" cried Hazel.

Just then, Posie's brother, Parsley, flew up.
Parsley had won an award at school, too.
In fact, he had won *all* the other awards.
"Tomorrow, I'm going to win the
Charmville Talent Show!" he bragged.

Lavender huffed as Parsley flew off. "Your big brother has a big head. What makes him so sure he will win the talent show?"

"Because he always wins everything," said Posie.

That gave Hazel an idea.

"Well, he's *not* going to win the talent show," she said. "You are!"

"I am?" Posie asked.

"Yes. You are the best flute player in Charmville," said Lavender.

"You deserve to win," said Hazel. "Lavender and I will help you! To the Charmhouse!"

The Little Charmers raced
to the Charmhouse.
Posie needed to practice her
flute before the show!
She played a sweet tune for
her friends.

"Perfectly pretty as always, Posie," said Hazel.

"Thank you!" said Posie.

"But that's the problem," Hazel said.

"To win, you need to give them something *flashy*!" Hazel said.

She charmed up a rock star outfit for Posie.

"A little splash to add some flash!" Hazel said. "Rock the Charmhouse!"

Posie played her flute again, faster this time.

It sounded charmtastic!

But Posie didn't think so.

"Sorry," she said. "This just isn't me."

"Maybe you could join me for the talent show. Then it could be *us*!" Posie said.

"What do you mean?" asked Lavender.

"I want my best friends rocking with me," said Posie.

"We'll do it!" cried Hazel and Lavender.

The friends charmed up a guitar, keyboard, and drums.

"I've got the perfect band name," said Posie. "Rainbow Sparkle!"

The Little Charmers were excited to play as a band!
But their music was all wrong.
The beat was off. The tune was flat.
In fact, it sounded . . .
"Bad," the friends said together.

"We *could* sound a lot better with a bit of help," said Hazel.

She held up her wand.

"You want to use magic?" Posie asked. "Is that fair?"

"It's not cheating to take music lessons,"
said Hazel. "Think of it as one big music
lesson."

"Okay," said Posie. "Let's do it! Sparkle up,
Charmers!"

"Cast a spell to help us win
as Rainbow Sparkle, we begin.
Playing in a group of three
as Rainbow Sparkle, that's the key!"

Poof! Hazel, Lavender, and Posie played their instruments again.

This time, they rocked!

They practiced all over town.

Treble, Flare, and Seven got into the groove, too.

"We sound great!" cried Posie.
"Especially you, Posie," said Hazel.
"That trophy has your name on it."

The next evening, all of
Charmville gathered for the
talent show.

Everyone was excited to see
the different acts!

First, two ogres tap-danced to
a jazzy tune.

Next, a group of frogs croaked out a magical music number.

Hazel's mom was one of the judges. "Nicely done," she said.

But the best act was Parsley.
He sang an awesome pop tune.
The audience went wild!

Backstage, Hazel was worried.
The other acts were *really* good.
"If we're going to win, we'll need a booster spell," she said.
"That doesn't seem fair," said Posie.

But Hazel didn't listen.
"I'll just ask for a little more
talent," she promised.

*"Abra-ca-doo, abra-ca-door,
make us rock out even more!"*

Poof! The Little Charmers hit the stage!

Hazel jammed on her guitar.

Lavender beat a rocking rhythm on the drums.

Posie's fingers twinkled across the keyboard.

The Little Charmers sounded more charmazing than ever!

"Wow," said Parsley. "I can't believe they're so good!"

"*Hmm*," said Hazel's mom. "Neither can I." She had a feeling something was up.

Then the spell began to wear off. "Uh-oh," said Hazel. "We need one more spell!"

"Fix our music, rhythm and words. Make our trio sing like birds!"

POOF!

Hazel's spell worked a bit *too* well.

The Little Charmers began to sing like chickens!

Cluck! Cluck! Cluck!

The audience laughed.
They thought it was part of the act!
That gave Posie an idea.
She and her friends did a chicken dance.
They finished their song with squawks!

At the end of the show, Hazel's mom counted the votes.

It was close . . . but Parsley won!

"Thanks!" he said. "I have to give a hand to Rainbow Sparkle. My sister and her friends were charmazing."

"Posie, come out and show everybody how you play the flute," said Parsley.

Posie smiled. "Absolutely!"

It was nice knowing her big brother was proud of her!

"I'm sorry I tried to take a talent show shortcut," Hazel said. "I guess I learned magic isn't the right way to win."

"It's okay," said Posie. "It was a talent show to remember.

Squawk!"